LULU IS A BLACK SHEEP

CASSANDRA GAISFORD

DEDICATION

For the sensitive children and adults
I have counselled
You inspire me

1
___

Once upon a time there was a little black sheep. Her hair was black as coal.

And everything that Lulu did her family disapproved.

They shamed Lulu to her face.

They criticised her behind her back.

They were cold, and critical, and constantly put her down.

And they always looked at her with a heavy, dark, frown.

2

Lulu tried to make them love her.

Lulu tried to make them happy.

Lulu tried to please them.

She tried to be like the rest of the flock.

She tried to be a little white sheep.

Here a baaaa. There a baaaa. Everywhere a baaaa. Baaaa!

But what she really wanted to say was "Yippee! Wow-wee! All the things we can be!"

But she kept her mouth shut.

She tried to make her fleece go white.

She tried to come out of the shadows.

But every time Lulu did, her family bellowed. And they threw her back.

"Why are you being mean to me?" she asked.

"There's something wrong with you," they snapped.

3
───────

One night when Lulu woke up she felt lonely and sad. She sat in the darkness because the black and the stillness always made her feel glad.

Night-time when everyone else was in bed was the time she loved best.

Suddenly Lulu heard a shrill, sharp, sound.

Squark! Squark! Squark!

She ran to the window and saw a funny looking bird in the bush. She went for a walk in her pyjamas and stumbled upon a nest.

"Who are you? Lulu asked.

"I'm a kiwi," the little bird replied.

"Birds are supposed to fly," Lulu said.

"I don't want to be like other birds," the kiwi said.

4

"Why are you out on your own? Don't you get lonely? Don't you feel sad?" Lulu asked

"No. Never," the kiwi said. "Nobody bothers me. I can do what I like. I can roam freely in the night."

"But you still can't fly," Lulu said. "Doesn't it worry you that people will say you're not quite right?"

"I don't listen. I don't care. They're not right. I know who I am, and I love myself with all my might."

Lulu listened and Lulu learned and Lulu loved the kiwi in the black.

"I can jump high, high, high into the sky. I can see in the dark. I can run fast, fast, fast. I can call out to other kiwis who are just like me."

And Lulu started to think. It's not who I am that matters.. It's remembering and focusing and believing on what I can do and what I've got.

She began to make a mental list. I am kind. I am generous. I am spiritual. I am creative. I live in a beautiful home. I grow vegetables of my own. I love spending time alone.

Lulu thought about all the unkind things her family had said. And she turned those thoughts right on their head.

6

———

W hat are you doing?" the kiwi laughed.

"I'm thinking upside down," Lulu said as she stood on her head. "When someone say something unkind, or does something mean I'm going to look at it a different way."

"Don't forget to move away," the kiwi said. " I never stay if there is danger ahead. "I jump high, high, high into the sky. I run fast, fast, fast. I run somewhere else to have my fun."

Lulu listened and Lulu wondered and Lulu thought.

"Do you think there's others out there like me?"

"Beautiful black sheep?" the kiwi asked.

"Uhh-huhhh," Lulu nodded.

"If you don't shout out you'll never know."

Lulu gave it a go.

L ulu Googled 'black sheep in the family'."
She found lots and lots and lots of help immediately.

She discovered lots of people were treated differently, disapproved of and excluded by their family.

She learned that black sheep had different values and beliefs.

She read about ways to cope and stay resilient.

And she learned that it was important to seek support from other communication networks—not just the Internet.

8

Lulu began to invest time in the relationships that were genuine and loving.

She focused on people who wanted to include her.

She turned her thoughts away from unkind people who made her hurt.

She sought support from her adoptive and chosen families and friends.

And she focused on the positive aspect of the challenges she faced being marginalised by her family of birth.

9

When others went low, she went high.

When they were mean, she was kind.

When people withheld their love she learned to love herself instead.

"Black is beautiful," she affirmed.

Black is strong.

Black is wonderful.

Without black there would be no night.

Without black there would no white.

Black absorbs all the light.

There is absolutely nothing wrong with black.

One day her family came back. They were kind, and loving, and bought her sweets.

But then . . .

They started being mean all over again.

Lulu decided she needed to support herself. She wanted to be self-reliant in case her family disowned her again and excluded her from their mob.

She did well in school and sought higher education so she could get a good job.

11

Lulu discovered that thinking upside down and reframing negatives into positives help the pain swirl around and around and around. All her hurts left her body and fell with a WHACK! to the ground.

Night by night she became stronger and stronger and stronger. She let go of the need for people to see everything through her eyes.

Stronger at saying no to bullying behaviour.

Stronger at saying no to trying to change them.

Stronger at saying no to wishing she was white.

Stronger at saying yes, yes, yes to living in the light.

12

___

Lulu said, yes, yes, yes to channelling her childhood experiences into something positive. Something with ZING!

She wrote stories, and created paintings, and drawings, and songs that made her heart sing.

She wrote books that made her heart glad.

She taught what she had learned.

"Own your power. Love yourself no matter what."

Her favourite thing of all was learning to live authentically, despite her family's disapproval.

"Dare to act, dare to dream, dare to be who and what you truly are," she told her little black sheep when they were born.

And to her little baby with the bright pink hair, she whispered, "You are special just as you are."

* * * THE END * * *

AUTHOR'S NOTE

This book was inspired by the realisation that I too am a black sheep. I've never felt I belonged in my family. I was always, and still am, criticised, shunned, and blamed when I don't walk to their beat. And I'm nearly 55 years young!

Sometimes they're good. And sometimes they're not. But love them anyway, and I've learned to act in a different way.

I woke in the night in the early hours of day three of the COVID-19 lockdown in New Zealand, and I heard a kiwi outside.

Hearing the kiwi call out last night, reminded me that they must feel like black sheep too. Our national birds are not like other birds. They have funny bodies, are nocturnal and they cannot fly. I love that kiwis embrace who they are and don't try to change.

They've learned to adapt to stay alive, and at night they forage, and shuffle, and sing with great happiness and joy.

I created this book for my younger self. I made this book for you and your children. I wrote this book with love, and happiness, and glee.

Read this book at bedtime, at times of stress or pain or joy! I hope you find this book a great treasure trove of comfort. This book is always here for you—no matter what!

Stay in your bubble, dear readers. Follow your truth. But most of all, keep being your beautiful self.

Much love

Cassandra

P.S. LULU IS a Black Sheep is now available in audio from all great online bookstores.

ABOUT THE AUTHOR

CASSANDRA GAISFORD is best known as *The Queen of Uplifting Inspiration.*

She is a holistic therapist, award-winning artist, and #1 bestselling author. A corporate escapee, she now lives and works from her idyllic lifestyle property overlooking the Bay of Islands in New Zealand.

Cassandra's unique blend of business experience and qualifications (BCA, Dip Psych.), creative skills, and wellness and holistic training (Dip Counselling, Reiki Master Teacher) blends pragmatism and commercial savvy with rare and unique insight and out-of-the-box-thinking for anyone wanting to achieve an extraordinary life.

ALSO BY THE AUTHOR

Stories and Fairytales

The Little Princess

I Have to Grow

The Little Boy Who Cried

The Little Princess Can Fly

Lulu Lost Her Confidence

Billy is a Balloon

Non-fiction Self-Empowerment Books

Mid-Life Career Rescue

How to Find Your Passion and Purpose

Bounce: Overcoming Adversity, Building Resilience and Finding Joy

Anxiety Rescue: How to Overcome Anxiety, Panic, and Stress and Reclaim Joy

Boost Your Self-Esteem and Confidence

No! Why 'No' is the New 'Yes'

More of Cassandra's practical and inspiring books on a range of life enhancing topics can be found on her website (www. cassandragaisford.com) and her author page at all good online bookstores.

ABOUT THE TRANSFORMATIONAL SUPER KIDS SERIES

From the bestselling author of *The Little Princess* comes a brilliant new series, *Transformational Super Kid*s.

These young heroes and heroines tackle modern-day problems with the passion and gusto of warriors.

They defeat cruel critics, they slay savage self-esteem demons, and they show people—jealous of their kindness, talent, and beauty—that their biggest superpower is staying true to themselves.

Suitable for 'kids' of all ages. After all, aren't we all still children at heart?

PRAISE FOR THE TRANSFORMATIONAL SUPERKIDS

"Delightful and uplifting. . .

Lulu is a black sheep is a delightful and empowering story for our times! Uplifting messages woven throughout. A feel good story most will relate to, especially grown ups! Another one to add to your collection of Cassandra's self empowerment books! Thank you Cassandra!Delightful and uplifting!"

~ Heather Dodge

"Being released from the trauma. . .

This story is about the gaining of true power in growing into one's true self through childhood pain, discovering a new way of being, and knowing how where to go to gain help with being released from the trauma that had become one boys life. It is in the Author's Notes that this story transforms from a book to help children into a valuable resource for therapist and others who work with boys of all ages. Cassandra has captured a very typical aspect of how many boys are parented and the resulting chaos that becomes their adult-self. For those of us fortunate enough to have the privilege of working with men (boys of all ages) this sad yet beautiful story is one to keep handy and to share broadly.

~ Catherine Sloan, Counselor and Intuitive Therapist

"Such a powerful message…

Sadly beautiful and a real reflection of our current society, which if we are really honest has lost direction, particularly with regards family values. Training in family values is an absolute pre-requisite before change will occur. I took pleasure in finding out the boy who cried not only survived but was blessed following the day the tears stopped and he found contentment, grace, and peace. My prayer is we can only attempt to save many more such boys."

~ Kenn Butler, CEO

"A wonderful tool…
This book is a wonderful tool for anyone seeking to begin the journey to self-reflection and healing from difficult child-hoods. Therapists will find this book useful for their patients young or old. To return as a child to discover where the source of the pain begins has always been valuable, but actually relating it to present day is key to understanding. Highly recommended."

~ Alma Hammond, Author

EXCERPT: THE LITTLE PRINCESS

PRAISE FOR THE LITTLE PRINCESS

"A Little Book with a Powerful Message...
An important reminder to always be true to yourself and
summon the courage to follow your passions... Only *you* can
live your life...GO live it!"

~ Harley

"The Little Princess is my hero…
I am a Midlife Coach, which means I help women find their
moxie to do what they might not have done in the first half of
their lives...I think *The Little Princess* needs to be a "required
reading" text book for us all...she cuts to the heart of the
lesson all of us need to hear, over and over again. *The Little
Princess* embodies courage. She is my hero."

~ Sheree Clarke, Midlife Courage Coach

***The Little Princess* is 'brilliant…**
Short concise & full of tremendous vision & wisdom,
expressed lovingly. Many of the comments read true for my

own journey. I recognise my passion to be different than many others, my persistence to succeed, & the pure joy I have at the end of each day when I lay down my head & give thanks."

~ Kenn Butler, CEO

"Very uplifting and inspiring…
I love everything Cassandra writes, the queen of uplifting inspiration! This is a little book, the story basically teaches you to have faith in your dreams, stand firm and don't let others rain on your parade.. We are all searching for purpose and passion, everybody hurts and sometimes we find ourselves on the receiving end of somebody else's insecurities, when they project their anger, jealousy etc onto us.. The old woman who puts the little princess down is really just jealous and stuck in her own life."

~ Reviewer UK

"A reminder of the truth in all of us…
The Little Princess is a great short story as a reminder of the truth in all of us; Don't judge, take loving kindness as a guideline in life, but stay true to yourself; A powerful message! Like all the books by this author, it is a guideline to live a wise life."

~ Maartje Jager, Designer

1

Once upon a time there was a young woman who wanted to make a difference in the world.

She wanted to help others. She wanted to help people overcome depression, anxiety, and feeling sad.

She wanted to to help them feel inspired, joyful and happy.

She just wasn't sure how.

One day she had an inspired idea. "I can help people find their passion and purpose," she thought.

Her heart fluttered then soared higher and higher and higher—far, far, far away.

Almost beyond the reach of her doubts and fears.

3

S he felt so excited—but also scared. She decided to feel the fear and create something anyway.

She knew people often struggled to find the time to read, and she wanted to make it easy and fun for people to find inspiration and help.

She decided to design a pack of inspirational cards that would enable people to help themselves and become empowered to transform their lives.

The cards would give people ideas, encourage them to dream, and give them hope.

4

She thought about the angel cards that had given her so much relief when she was an anxious child.

"Wouldn't it be fun to create something similar?" she thought.

Each card would have an inspirational quote on one side and a self-help strategy on the other.

DID YOU ENJOY THIS EXCERPT?

Grab your own copy of *The Little Princess.*
Follow your heart! Heed the call for courage.

Feeling stuck, depressed or demotivated? There are so many reasons why you should follow your dreams. If you need some motivation, look no further than this book.

Part moral allegory and part spiritual autobiography, *The Little Princess* is a timeless charm which tells the story of a young woman who leaves the safety of fitting in with everyone else, to follow her heart.

Be inspired by this journey to transformation and self-acceptance, and self-belief as she learns to overcome the vagaries of adult behaviour. Her personal odyssey culminates in a voyage of self-belief, passion, and purpose.

From the best-selling author of Mid-Life Career Rescue, Stress Less and How to Find Your Passion and Purpose: a powerful, inspiring, and practical book about boosting resilience, overcoming obstacles and moving forward after life's inevitable setbacks.

Find out what strategies are sabotaging your success. Find and follow your passion and purpose faster.

The Little Princess is available in audio, eBook, Hardcover and Paperback from all great online retailers.

COPYRIGHT

The intent of the author is only to offer information of a general nature to help you in your quest for emotional, physical, and spiritual well-being.

Any use of information in this book is at the reader's discretion and risk. Neither the author nor the publisher can be held responsible for any loss, claim or damage arising out of the use, or misuse, of the suggestions made, the failure to take medical advice or for any material on third party websites.

First published by Blue Giraffe Publishing 2020

ISBN PRINT: 978-1-99-002027-8
ISBN EBOOK: 978-1-99-002028-5